Andrew Barber

Trucks

Illustrated by Karl Pitwon

OXFORD
UNIVERSITY PRESS

This book belongs to

OXFORD
UNIVERSITY PRESS

Great Clarendon Street, Oxford OX2 6DP

Oxford University Press is a department of the University of Oxford.
It furthers the University's objective of excellence in research, scholarship,
and education by publishing worldwide in

Oxford New York

Athens Auckland Bangkok Bogotá Buenos Aires
Cape Town Chennai Dar es Salaam Delhi Florence Hong Kong Istanbul
Karachi Kolkata Kuala Lumpur Madrid Melbourne Mexico City Mumbai
Nairobi Paris São Paulo Shanghai Singapore Taipei Tokyo Toronto Warsaw

Oxford is a registered trade mark of Oxford University Press
in the UK and in certain other countries

First published 2001

Hardback ISBN 0-19-910624-X
Paperback ISBN 0-19-910625-8

3 5 7 9 10 8 6 4 2

Printed in Spain by Edelvives.

Contents

▶ Trucks around the world

It's midnight. In the quiet of the
Australian desert, a rumbling noise
begins. It gets louder – and
LOUDER. Along comes a huge
shape, blazing with light. It's the
longest truck on the road!
Australians call it a road train.

snow collection truck   snow-blower

It's morning. In a Canadian town, it's been snowing. Snow lies everywhere. Along comes a snow-blower. A whirling drum at the front sucks up snow, then – whoosh – blows it into a waiting truck.

It's afternoon. In Pakistan, a beautifully decorated truck climbs a mountain road. It's carrying food, petrol cans, chickens – a hundred things!

▶ Trucks!

Trucks! They're big. They're powerful.

breakdown truck

delivery truck

Trucks are stronger than a hundred horses. They can carry heavy loads for thousands of miles.

concrete mixer

ore
carrier

dumper truck

You don't drive to the shops in a truck, or take it on holiday. Trucks have work to do.

Trucks move things from place to place – but that's not all. There are trucks that mix concrete, trucks that clean the streets, trucks with cranes on them and trucks for putting out fires.

▶ Two kinds of truck

Any truck has to be one of two kinds
– rigid or articulated.

Smaller trucks are RIGID.

The cab, where the driver sits, and
the body, the part that carries the
load, are all in one piece.

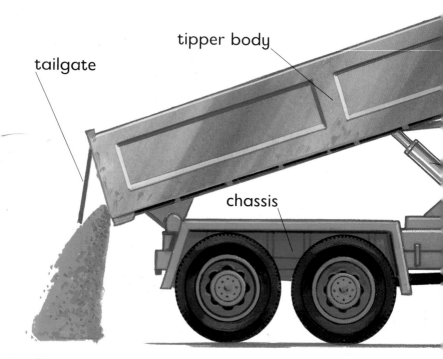

tipper body

tailgate

chassis

Rigid trucks have a strong frame, called a chassis. Different kinds of truck have different bodies fastened to the chassis. So rigid trucks can do all kinds of different jobs. Tipper trucks carry things like sand or gravel. To unload, the body tips up.

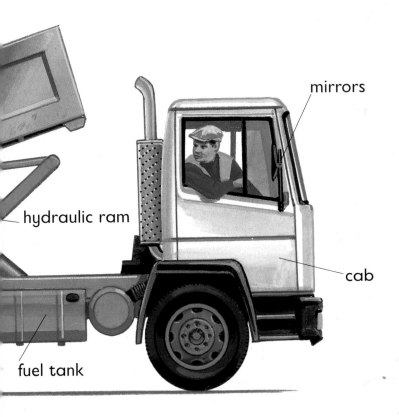

mirrors

hydraulic ram

cab

fuel tank

Long trucks can carry bigger loads. But if they are rigid, it's hard to steer round tight corners. To make things easier, long trucks are ARTICULATED!

mirrors

cab

fuel tank

This means that the truck is in two pieces – the cab and the trailer. On corners, the truck can bend at the "fifth wheel", where the cab and trailer join.

fifth wheel

trailer

▶ Truck checklist

Before a long trip, a truck has to be checked over to make sure everything works properly. Let's look at the driver's checklist.

✓ **Brakes**
To get a heavy truck moving, you need a powerful engine. To stop it, you need powerful brakes! The driver checks that the trailer's brake pipes are connected properly.

fifth wheel

reversing lights

Engine

Diesel, oil and water – the engine needs them all. Diesel is the fuel that keeps the engine going. Oil stops it from seizing up. Water keeps the engine cool.

connections to trailer brakes and lights

fuel tank

engine

Lights

Do all the lights work? Headlights, tail lights, reversing lights, indicator lights – the driver checks them all.

Load

The trailer is loaded with boxes and boxes of food. If the boxes are not loaded properly, the truck will be hard to steer.

indicator light

tail light

tail lift

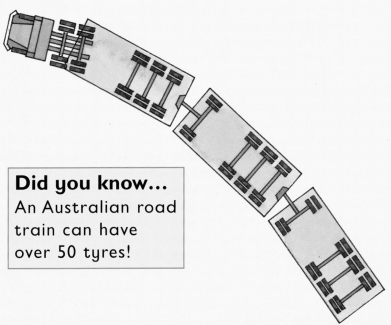

Did you know...
An Australian road train can have over 50 tyres!

Now the truck is ready to go. The driver climbs in. He turns the ignition key and the engine starts with a roar. The journey has begun.

load

✓ **Tyres**
A truck has more wheels than a car. The heavier the load it has to carry, the more wheels it needs. If a tyre is soft, or the tread is worn, it could cause an accident.

removal truck

low-loader

▶ On the motorway

The truck heads for the motorway.
First stop is a supermarket, far to the
north.

The driver sees a low-loader. It's
carrying a very heavy load – a huge
bulldozer.

milk tanker

dividing wall

Behind the low-loader is a milk tanker. The big tank on the back is divided up into smaller parts. This stops the liquid from sloshing about too much.

A removal truck is taking a family's belongings to their new home. Everything is padded and carefully strapped down.

There's a hold-up ahead. A new bridge is being built, and the road works are causing a traffic jam.

WHOOMPH!

A digger tips a load of earth into a dumper truck. A big dumper can carry the weight of 50 elephants.

bulldozer

dumper truck   digger

One of the road workers is talking into a radio. "Left a bit… stop! OK, bring it down." A mobile crane lowers part of the bridge into place.

mobile crane

▶ Delivering the goods

The truck has come many miles since morning. But it has reached the supermarket at last. A fork-lift truck unloads boxes and crates.

The driver is tired. He can't drive
home tonight. But he doesn't need
anywhere to stay – he has everything
in the cab!

The driver pulls into a truck stop and
settles down for the night.

Trucks at night

The delivery truck has finished its day's work. But other trucks are still working. Trucks often travel at night, because the roads are less busy.

A truck carrying frozen food drives through the night. The back is like a giant fridge.

refrigerated truck

car transporter

A transporter goes the other way, piled high with cars. There's room on board for eleven cars.

Along comes a container truck, going to the docks. At the docks, the truck doesn't need to unload. A huge crane lifts the whole container off the truck.

container truck

▶ Tough trucks

For a tough job, you need a tough truck. Some trucks are built to work in all weathers, on rough tracks as well as on roads.

A rugged truck bounces along a forest track, carrying a huge load of logs. The logs are headed for the sawmill, to be cut into planks.

Two trucks meet in the middle of an icy wasteland in Alaska, USA. They are both carrying oil-drilling equipment. It's so cold that the fuel tanks must be heated to stop the diesel from freezing.

▶ Emergency

If there's a fire, or the telephone lines break, or a street light goes out, trucks can help. You can rely on trucks in an emergency.

E E E A A A W !

Fire trucks rush to a fire, carrying hoses, water and other equipment. In no time, firefighters are aiming powerful jets of water at the flames.

fire tender

hydraulic ram

platform
truck

▶ Trucks on show

Trucks are built to work – but a few are used for fun!

Stunt trucks have **ENORMOUS** wheels. They do wheelies, and drive over piles of wrecked cars.

stunt truck

The wheels of a drag truck spin madly as it starts, and the front lifts right off the ground. Then it shoots away, leaving a smell of fuel and burnt rubber.

drag truck

The last truck has gone – the audience get in their cars and head for home. On the way they pass trucks of all kinds, on many different journeys.

Glossary

This glossary will help you to understand what some important words mean. You can find them in this book by using the page numbers given below.

 body The body is the back part of a rigid truck, where the load is carried. **8, 9**

 brake pipe Brake pipes are connections from the brake pedal inside a car or truck to the brakes on the wheels. **12**

 delivery truck A delivery truck is used for trips with lots of stops. The sides often open for easy access. **22**

 fork-lift truck A fork-lift truck has a special carrier on the front for lifting crates. **20**

ignition key The key that starts up a truck or car is called the ignition key. **15**

 low-loader A low-loader is a truck with a low platform at the back. It is designed to carry extra-large or heavy loads. **16, 17**

 trailer The trailer is the back part of an articulated truck, where the load goes. **11, 12, 14**

 tread A tyre has a pattern of grooves and ridges called the tread, which help it grip the road. **15**

 truck stop Truck stops are places where truck drivers can park safely and get a drink and something to eat. **21**

Reading Together

Oxford Reds have been written by leading children's authors who have a passion for particular non-fiction subjects. So as well as up-to-date information, fascinating facts and stunning pictures, these books provide powerful writing which draws the reader into the text.

Oxford Reds are written in simple language, checked by educational advisors. There is plenty of repetition of words and phrases, and all technical words are explained. They are an ideal vehicle for helping your child develop a love of reading – by building fluency, confidence and enjoyment.

You can help your child by reading the first few pages out loud, then encourage him or her to continue alone. You could share the reading by taking turns to read a page or two. Or you could read the whole book aloud, so your child knows it well before tackling it alone.

Oxford Reds will help your child develop a love of reading and a lasting curiosity about the world we live in.

Sue Palmer
Writer and Literacy Consultant